EAT THE COOKIE

by Jim Lowenstern

RoseDog Books
PITTSBURGH, PENNSYLVANIA 15238

RoseDog Books
585 Alpha Drive, Suite 103
Pittsburgh, PA 15238
Visit our website at *www.rosedogbookstore.com*

ISBN: 979-8-88925-263-4
eISBN: 979-8-88925-763-9

Mary Montgomery looked out the window as the rain poured down. Puddles were forming on what had once been a street. As long as Mary had lived on Cabots Lane, she couldn't remember the street being paved. Maybe ten years ago, the government did those poor people a favor by paving the road. *Brrrinng,* the phone rang. Mary picked up the classic styled bronze phone.

"Hello Mary, this is Ethel."

"Ethel, how are you? Dreadful weather we're having. It's been two weeks, hasn't it?"

"Mary, I have a problem. Do you know my check hasn't come in?"

"They're always late these days."

"Mary, my check is green."

"Oh that means it is two weeks late."

"Mary, I've got to eat."

"Ethel, why don't you go to the welfare center?"

"I did Wednesday. I got the run around. 'Your check, madamm should come in the mail today.' Those bastards, Oh, how polite those bastards act. I said to him, 'My check is one week and three days late. My husband and children have to eat.' 'Madam, this all the time I can give you.' This other brute then escorted me to the door. The lines are so long, just for the run around. All my friends with green checks haven't received them either. Mary, could you go to the center for me?"

"Well Ethel, I don't know."

"I just want my check. I tried to do it myself, but I think you can get it for me. Look Mary, my ride is here. We're going to the country, maybe we'll find something."

"Maybe. Good luck Ethel, I'll go to the center before it closes tonight. Bye."

"Goodbye."

Mary put the earphone on the hook. She leaned back on the red leather lounge sinking into the soft cushion. She wondered where Richard was and if she had been too hard on him. The boy didn't want to go to school or work. *I tried, I tried,* she thought as she looked across the room at Richard's high school graduation picture. He had blue eyes, short well-kept hair, a compact but square jaw. He once had such aspirations. A lawyer, he was going to be a lawyer.

Crack.

Mary's head shook out of her dream. She bolted up and ran to the window. She saw a bunch of youth gesturing at a police car that had just fired a shot. She looked for a dead body but there wasn't any. Just as well, a warning shot. Mary glanced at the grandfather clock it was 4:30. She had until 6:00 to get to the welfare office.

She went over to the closet, opened it, and stared at all of her coats. *For such a bad day, maybe I should wear this awful coat my son gave me. What is it, a pea coat?* Mary slipped her coat on and went out the door.

Outside, the rain had lessened but the wind had whipped up. Mary walked at a furious pace for two blocks until she made her bus stop. She was the only person standing by the sign, while down the road eighty yards, about thirty people were in a sheltered plexiglass bus stop.

Mary found the highest point on the sidewalk to avoid the puddles. Her legs straddled two feet. The rain began to come down harder. An empty bus came down Independence Ave, but it was a white bus and Mary knew that it would only pick up at the sheltered bus stop.

As the driver approached Mary, he seemed to slow down. The mustachioed bus driver stared at Mary, his eyes wide and widened as he got closer. Instead of turning away, Mary became incensed and began to glare at him. The last possible instant she saw him, his mouth was hanging open and a dumbfounded look on his face. Mary watched as the bus picked up all the people, who started to turn their heads at the lone person at the bus stop. Each one of them now was staring at Mary.

Mary could see eyes until the bus was out of view. During this time, Mary's anger had turned to bewilderment. *Why are they staring at me?*

A few seconds later came a bus twenty years older, with a peeling black paint job. It creaked and squeaked as it pulled up to pick her up. Mary boarded. She saw a ruddy complexioned Irishman, his hair was a dull red. He sprouted a few days growth. He kept looking at Mary's clothes. When Mary passed him, she heard him mutter, "Gucci." Mary looked down at her shoes as she took a seat in the middle of the empty bus.

Mary stared out of her window at an elderly gentleman in a tweed suit, smoking a pipe. He waved to her. Mary smiled, it was nice for such an attractive man to wave to her. The bus turned off Independence Ave and hit Lancaster St, a more modern part of town. Mary reacquainted herself with all the buildings. The bus stopped at the orthodox influenced Mantequilla building with its famous dome and arches and vaults. The bus became fuller after that next stop.

Two young working women took the seat in front of Mary. They glanced at her as she stared out the window, one girl then broke into Mary's world.

"Haven't I seen you before?"

Mary whirled her head at the assailant.

"Aren't you...?"

"No," Mary snorted at the red-haired woman.

The red-haired woman's face flushed. She regained her composure then, as she smacked her lips, winked to her friend, and gave a tight smile.

As Mary was turning her head away.

"Charlie is going to Gooseland to shoot some deer this weekend."

"Ann, why isn't he going to Kandati?"

"It's too far away. Besides, he can safely stay at his parents. He can't get in any trouble hitchhiking. Look, it's the perfect alibi. Not only that, Toni, I hear out there the road problem isn't as bad as it is here. It so bad he couldn't drive a car and bring some food back."

"Ann, you know Chuck lost his car when the car tax came, the same as Ronny did, the same as everyone Chuck and I know."

"Don't you know anyone? I mean Gooseland that is an opportunity for so many people to be helped out."

"We tried to ask around for a car two months ago. I don't know. It's not like you can call over the telephone. Ann, I told a lot of people, but nothing has ever come through."

"How much do you think he'll bring back?"

"Just some deer in the suit, in the lining, sewn up and wrapped in foil and deodorized with a dash of white pepper, so the dogs won't smell."

"Won't he bring some vegetables back? That is a trip to Gooseland wasted. Why doesn't Charles bring a bag of tomatoes and corn back?"

"Ann, they check people hitchhiking."

"Not everyone."

"They still do. You can't smuggle food. Charles isn't in jail."

"Toni, sometimes you gotta take risks. How are Danny and Patty going to stay healthy?"

"They get plenty of vitamins and supplements. Ann, I am tired of talking about food. Anyway, at least we are lucky we live in Lawrence Province."

"Why? You mean the water?"

"Yes, let's see, Kingston got poisoned last Thursday. Mosquito diss..."

"Malaria."

"Yes, Newton has a mutant disease, what is it, Ann?"

"It hits the lungs first and I don't think it's mutant. It's asthma poisoning, that's all...."

"Proctorville has the common cold, probably Uncle Sully called last night, He is sure its the water. Why hasn't the government done anything about it."

"They did at two o'clock today. The epidemic hasn't yet reached Elizabethtown, I wonder why they did it."

The bus stopped and the two younger women got off.

Mary always listened to conversations on buses. She never got in any herself. You could see so much about other people, listening to their conversations. See what interested and troubled people, and look out the window. Listen to people and look out the window. Out a window, you could see a live movie. Adults reliving their childhood fantasies, lovers quarreling. Mary loved most seeing people's emotions. The situations that would bring out the worst in people, to see if people can contain their anger.

Mary's head was still placed outside the window when two men sat in front of her.

"Jeremy, my my it's so fine we got together. You know it;s been so long since we last saw each other, why did they have to transfer you?"

"Earl, it's hard on me. Have you been lonely?"

"Well, no Jer…"

"Then Earl look, I'm back with you. Let's make the best of the vacation."

"Is it really a vacation? My gosh Jeremy, I hope this isn't some government trick."

"Relax Earl; I'm a specialist. They couldn't find someone to take my place. Remember, I'm training people to replace, Earl. You know they are the dumbest bunch of clods I have ever seen. Really Earl, doesn't all of what is going on in this country bore you? 'Oh I can't get any food.' 'My black market sources have dried up.' 'I can't drink the water.'"

"Stop Jeremy, I don't expect you to talk like those common clods, even if you're being sarcastic. Let's talk about something interesting."

"Earl, I had the weirdest dream last night."

"What did it have to with?"

"Feces."

"Jeremy."

"Seriously Earl, did you ever think movie stars have diarrhea? What is their diarrhea like?"

"Well, sure they do. Like when it gets hot in the anus and you hear pebbles hitting in the middle of the lake, sometimes it is and almost sounds like urine, thin sounding. How about when you have such an intense pain when you try to have a movement..."

Mary was so glad it was time for her to get off. She pulled at the cord above her head. *Queers, gross queers.*

The bus pulled to a stop and Mary walked back and exited through the rear door. *It's funny, the queers weren't bores, but it is good to get off the bus, so I don't have to listen to that rubbish. I wonder where my son is?*

A blonde-haired young man was rotating his penis in the rear end of a muscular brown-haired man. The blonde was corkscrewing his penis deeper and deeper. The brown-haired man pressed his toes deep into the bed as he tightened his buttocks. He then released his buttocks then snapped his rear as hard as he could at the blonde man on top. The blonde tightened his grip on the biceps of the brown-haired man. He then shoved his penis as hard as he could, to the depths of his partner's rectum. The brown-haired man let out a gasp while the blonde caressed the brown-haired with the left hand and tingled the nipple with the right hand. The two men made love on an enormous bed inside an eight man tent. Four lights were suspended from the corners of the square tent top, all spotlighting at one point in the middle of the bed, the center point of the tent. The shag rug to the sides of the tent were portable heaters. A table stood at the closed end of the tent, with a picture on it of a woman with grey hair, brown eyes, and a very beautiful face.

Mary is given 1071 and sat in the chair designated for her by the social worker. The welfare building always reminded her of a warehouse. But today it was packed with people who needed its use and the building seemed smaller. Mary had been getting strange looks all day. One lady she had never seen before said hello to her as if she knew her. Or that man who came up to her and began giving her a dissertation about the state of affairs in the government. Luckily, the line to the registrar moved fast, so she didn't have to pay attention to those strange people.

She was by a couple of young men on one side.

"I ate some limburger cheese and rye crisp as a laxative."

"Limburger cheese is no laxative, you fool. Try prunes."

"I don't like prunes."

"Who likes prunes? You don't eat them for pleasure; you eat them for necessity."

"Not everyone. Prune eaters eat prunes."

"Well, why don't you get some prunes after we get through with this mess?"

"I don't know. What else works like prunes?"

"Raisins."

"No, I don't like their taste."

"Well, I guess other fruits do almost as well."

"I don't like to eat fruit. I'm a meat and potato man."

"No wonder you're always constipated."

"Constipated, what's that?"

"Constipated, when you can't do a bowel movement."

"Bowel movement, does that have anything to do with taking a crap?"

"How do you expect to have one if you don't take a true laxative or fruit?" The only thing limburger cheese will is smell up the place. Besides limburger, well cheeses in general, cause liquid feces."

"Fisses?"

"God damn it."

"Oh, I understand. The thing is I like liquid fisses."

"But they are so hot and gooey and uncomfortable."

"I had hard fisses about a month ago. It was like they were too big for my asshole."

"Anus."

"They hurt as they come out. The pain was incredible."

"Oh, that happens to all of us."

"But I don't like that happening to me. I would rather have soft fisses."

"feeeecccceeessss."

"I have had soft feces for the last month. Whenever I feel a hard one come on, I try to hold it in so hopefully it will turn soft."

"Jeez."

"Why crap hard when you can crap soft?"

"Oh."

"No, I ate the richest food possible. I also drank a lot, that always helps."

"Drank what? Oh sorry, stupid question. Why can't you take a bowel movement like anyone else?"

"Because my asshole would hurt."

"God, does my anus hurt?" moaned the muscular, brown-haired man. "I was going to use Vaseline but you said no."

"I like pain. It was tight."

Today, Dick, you've got to admit, today was one of the best."

"Still, after it is over, I don't want you to be in pain, my bunny dear," as he hugged his bunny.

The two of them got out of bed and held on to each other. Bunny moved his fingers through Dick's hair. Dick grabbed an inch of Bunny's muscular buttock, and he brushed his other hand up Bunny's backbone to his neck. Bunny bent forward and sucked up a hunk of skin at the base of Dick's neck. Dick lowered his hand down Bunny's pelvis. He put his finger through Bunny's curls, drilling his way through the bush, close to the edge. He then grabbed Bunny's fallen angel, squeezing it with all his might. Bunny bit his lip as his penis shot up. Richard loosened his grip on the shaft and began stroking the head.

"Richard, why did you do that?"

"What are you talking about?"

"The smelly."

"I'm sorry. I farted Bunny"

"You know how much that repulses me, Richard. I think it is plain gross."

"Number 1071."

Mary is called and walked down the aisle of chairs, took a right, and went into the room with the red light over the door.

"Hello, I am Mr. Promiok. Please sit down. And what is your name my lady? Mary Montgomery?"

"Yes, that is right."

"I suppose your middle name is Louise."

"Why yes, it is."

"Mrs. Montgomery, I'm surprised you are still in this country."

"What's so funny about that, Mr. Promiok? I'm just an ordinary person, I demand to be treated that way."

"Oh, of course you are. What is it that is bothering you?"

"I have a friend who has a green check. She has not received it yet and I have a red check that is three days late."

"Mrs. Montgomery, your check should be at your doorstep tomorrow. A mail foul up, most people received their checks today."

"And the green check is a mail foul up too?"

"Well, Mrs. Montgomery, you are an intelligent person. Why should I try to snow you? Most people I have these set lines for. But you shall be different because even if you know the truth, you don't have the power for anything to matter. We aren't giving out green checks until Premier Badon Nabutu approves. The reason we aren't giving checks is for past historical performance by the old government. Don't get me wrong."

"Yes, I know what you are talking about. Is this the new government's plan? An eye for an eye, a tooth for a tooth, such as poison the water and starve the people?"

"I don't know anything about the water."

"Sure, you don't."

"If you knew the ill feelings Premier Badon Nabutu has toward these bizarre happenings. If he finds who is responsible, he will execute of wrong doing immediately."

"What's he going to do, beat himself to death? Thank you for your time, Mr. Promiok. I know where this government's position lies."

"Badon, will you get out of the bathroom?"

"I'm going to stay all day."

"Stop worrying about the white people's water. You didn't do it. Someone else did."

"Who did?"

"Badon, I have a big dinner for you. Come here. Relax, take your mind off of your worries."

"You know why I am here."

"You eat too fast, you don't relax. If you eat my dinner, you'll have your BM."

Nabutu forced the movement slowly. *Will we ever have a revolution? No one stops to think about the planning necessary to accomplish our goal. I don't want to align this country with one of the global giants or play for the friendship of all the super powers nor do I want to get in the little nations power struggle. This country can get strong by itself. It needs to do things alone at first to get strong. Everyone knows this country.*

Nabutu forced the movement slowly, but it wouldn't come. He sat very uncomfortably on the seat. All these years of muscle contractions had given him an uneasy feeling, either feces that felt like they would tear his anus apart or the farts or feces so soft that they would splatter.

Every bowel movement was an event. A victory to achieve, a splash in the bowl, a physical pain in the anus. It was special the time he had the perfect crap. A smooth, fast, long feces going out at good speed. Yet those were so rare.

Why couldn't I have married a girl who could cook the old fashioned way?

Badon felt a chill run through him, he shoved his hands the deepest they'd get in his worn-out field jacket. He was a funny sight wearing a coat, part of a military uniform for some nation nobody knew of, shivering in a drainage run off of a super highway, standing by himself instead of trying to belong at least to a small group.

Why did I have to come so early? It is one and a half hours before the meeting begins. I don't know anyone. I've got to speak when the meeting starts. Where is Blianto or Bludini?

He gathered his thoughts as he looked 200 yards up the tunnel. What are these black things? They look like stalactites. They are so thin, swaying to their own time. He reached up and touched the fifteen inch black drip. Gooey sticky mess.

Damn it, I've got this shit on my hands.

Badon whipped his hand down violently, trying to shake off the goo, then rubbed his finger. *What if I make a point with my finger and all the others can see is my gooey finger? Oh, it is cold. Will this stuff ever come off? Good, some of it is coming off.*

Badon was rubbing fanatically with his right-hand thumb and first finger. A few of the assembly were already looking at him.

A big fat man laughed at Badon's fortunes, "What happened, little boy? Got your hands dirty?"

Badon turned and stared at the man. After fifteen seconds of silence that affected those who had been watching, Badon turned away from the fat man, having not exchanged words, still rubbing his finger.

That was the right way, that obese thing. I didn't lose face. Stand up and be proud. I'm glad I didn't speak. He tried to make me look like a fool. Yet, I weathered him and gave him no fodder for a return volley.

The people had caught the fat man's remark and a few more who were curious at everything were still looking at Badon. Some out and out stared, some more cautiously, and a couple who saw the whole thing were laughing at the absurdity of the boy cleaning his fingers getting so much attention.

Blianto, Bludini, and I were all eating koshori at Blianto's apartment. We were listening to that awful Tambor folk music. Too many different rhythms for the same melody. Definite lack of harmony. Blianto would never hear any of it. We always spent a lot of time arguing. Bludini would just sit and look at the ceiling, walls, anything but us. Bludini was always bored by music, he'd rather hear the sweet sound of pulleys and cogs, the hum of machines. Blianto and I were arguing about this Tambor album, that it revolutionized Tanganyikan Jazz. I mean this was little much. Bludini had gone outside. Blianto and I continued to hurl insults at each other.

Daviary, Ralph Armstrong's military attache was an organization man. He was with a bomb specialist, Dashiki, who really didn't know as much as Blianto or me. It kind of jolted me seeing those two come in the apartment followed by Bludini, who resumed his open mouth staring at the ceiling. Blianto was having trouble breathing, his arguing was so fierce.

Then in came Albo, the old bald general, and Moagle, another saw-horse from the Of and Chancor wars. With the exception of Blianto, the room was silent. Albo took one glance at Blianto and turned and glared at Dashiki.

I broke the disturbing silence, "Tanganyikan music has a slight Zulu influence, but obviously Lantu and Diatu are the forefathers to Tanganyikan Jazz, and Dorcab String music."

"Cut the bullshit," Daviary bellowed.

Blianto's head nodded in agreement, "See? I am right."

"You ass, shut up," Daviary directed to Blianto and Nabutu, "You, Mr. Bludini, all of us came all the way here to talk about music."

"Tambor Folk music has nothing to do with Tanganyikan Jazz," I interjected.

"Let's leave now," Albo said, "we are obviously wasting our time."

"Patience Albo, what I and the others are about to tell you is very important. So, I hope all of you in this room can hold a reasonable discussion. First of all, this will come as a shock to all of you, Ralph Armstrong is dead. Mr. Nabutu, neither one of your aides has the backbone to rule this country. You, my friend, do. As you know nobody was designated to take over if Ralph Armstrong died. I will explain why I want you to be the leader. Mr. Albo and Mr. Dashiki were informed of my decision to ask you... though they do not agree totally. I will explain to you three for the first time and my army friends for the second time. I am second-in-command of the people's army. Now first-in-command. I guess that I could take the job of prime minister. Seriously, I don't have knowledge of economics or governmental organization. Ralph Armstrong unfortunately didn't have a tremendous amount of knowledge on these subjects either. But he didn't need to either. He had leadership, charisma, personality, and everyone liked him. He was smart enough to pick his friends and advisors. Mr. Nabutu, you were the main advisor to Ralph and you masterminded his political rise in the past well. You helped."

"Richard and Sam, are you there?"

"Be just a minute Earnest."

"Please hurry, it is urgent. Your doors are locked."

"Yes, that's right Ernie," Richard said. "Keep your pants on. No, take them off, now that I think about it."

"Richard, you devil."

The door was shaking violently, Richard unhooked the door, "Whew, it's cold Earnest."

"Put on a shirt Richard. As a matter of fact, try some pants, shoes, and a coat. The same goes for you Bunn... Sam."

"Are we going for a walk in the park?" Bunny giggled.

"Both of you know we have been tapping all communications systems around here. There have been two calls today to the police from farmers in the area claiming there are white people camping out in Geeseland."

"So, what's wrong with that? Just destroy all our equipment that might be..."

"No, maybe you're right Ernie," Bunny said, "Richard, we didn't hit Dorchester Province."

"Simple, my mother lives there."

"Yes, but the effect will only last two months or less."

"It's out of the question, I never planned to hit Dorchester."

"Madame Montgomery," the derelict said to Mary when she was ten feet away from him.

Mary gritted her teeth and stared at him.

"The greatest prime minister this country has known."

Mary blushed, though her face was still fierce. "Sir, that was thirteen years ago. I don't like to think about it anymore."

"After you did for those blackies, look what they did back to you."

"Well, unfortunately my successors didn't follow my example. Stopped the progress, let us say."

"You look like…"

Mary had actually stopped to talk to him.

"You're in a hurry, so God be with you."

"And with you."

"Badon, hasn't dinner been so pleasant?"

"Yes Jakata," Badon leaned over and to kiss his wife.

"Think this is the most you have eaten in a week. A good meal for a good man."

"Darling, it still worries me, about the white's water."

"Badon, please don't worry about your job. Look here's dessert.

Where are we going to go, Richard? The others, they've got places to go. Why did they have to destroy the tent? I have no parents; all my friends are out of this country."

"Don't worry Bunny, we are forty-five minutes away from a ride to my mother's."

"She's still in this country?"

"Yes."

"What's wrong with her? Isn't she living in a tenement?"

"Yes, yes, a wretched place. I'll have no more of your squalling. Come with me." Richard gave Bunny his hand.

Bunny squeezed it, "Okay babe, I know you'll lead me to the sun."

Mary sat on the bus all alone. She looked out the window watching the rain turn to snow. The trees looked so frail and tender with the snow covering them. It was wet snow, and a pleasant temperature outside. People were looking out the windows of their apartments. Some went out to their balcony; children were frolicking in the snow. A teenager cocked, aimed, and fired a snowball at the moving bus. The snowball burst right into Mary's window, ruining Mary's panorama.

The bus skidded to a stop.

"Luther, stop throwing snowballs at vehicles. Luther, do you hear me? Sir, you'll have to excuse my son."

"Don't worry you's mind, ma'am," the bus driver said.

"Hello... would it be all right if I sat beside you? I just have to talk to someone."

"Surely."

"I see you've met my son. He certainly is an excellent shot, throwing a snowball does no harm anyway. Look, it's already out of the window."

"He's just a little mischievous, with today's affairs, I can understand that."

"Jesus, that's the truth. How can I get him out of my hair?"

"Do you have any relatives in other countries?"

"No, even if I did, I wouldn't send my son there. This is my country. It's been good enough for me, it'll be good enough for him."

"But think of the education he could get over there."

"No one in my family has had an education past high school. We Anthonys are working people. The government just won't give him a job."

"They won't give any white person a job now. If I was younger, I'd be in another country because today, there is no opportunity here. I love this country, I'm sixty-five."

"Your sixty-five?"

"Yes."

"But you barely look fifty."

"Well, thank you. It's just that I'm an old lady and have a few years to live. I might as well live them here. But you've got forty years to live, you look strong and healthy. Why don't you go to a country where you can live in freedom?"

"Well, you two do what want, while I make some dinner."

"What are we having Mother?"

"It'll be a surprise."

"Richard, how could your mother keep this house this way?"

"She is a powerful woman."

"How about rich?"

"She is that too."

"What I thought the government took all our wealth away."

"From most people. Some people hide it better than others, some people the government gave gifts to."

"What they helped the blacks take over?"

"When they were in power, they helped the blacks. You're smart, you figure it out."

"But how does that fit in with your mother?"

"Mary Montgomery."

"Mary…"

"Was Prime Minister."

"Montgomery, that Mary Montgomery? Why isn't she in America, England, or somewhere far away?"

"Because she didn't want to go."

"She didn't have the money nor the means to move. All the moving companies blacklisted her."

"The Erder government offered to foot the bill for us to move, then the Nabutu government did, the White Shield, Kopach, and our man Ivan Doss."

"Ivan Doss…"

"From most people. Some people hide better than others, some people the government gave gifts to."

"What, they helped the blacks take over?"

"When they were in power, they helped the blacks. You're smart, figure it out."

"This is certainly a beautiful house."

"Bunny, are you on one of your interior decoration kicks again?"

"Richard, you are getting tense, why don't you relax?"

"I guess you're right Bunny," Richard reached over to kiss him, The two embraced for but a second.

"Richard, why don't you lie down on the couch and go to sleep, you could use a cat nap."

"Okay babe."

"Boys, dinner is ready."

"Mother," Samuel said, "Where do you get those chops? They're so big. You can't get chops in a store like that anymore."

"Oh Samuel, I don't like to talk about where I get my furniture or my food or anything. I just do. Well Richard, why have you come back after these years?"

"Don't you remember Mother? You kicked me out."

"Yes, but I didn't want to kick you out, but what could I do? Nineteen years old, you didn't want to go to work or go to school. It seemed you were living a hedonistic experience. Didn't you like girls back then?"

"Yeah, I wanted to love a girl... but no girl would love me."

"Just because you couldn't, let's say, get it on with debutantes, you gave up on women?"

"But don't you see I like men better than women because I can be myself: I don't have to play games. Relations are out in the open. Bunny, could you try to?"

"Sure I will. Mrs. Montgomery, I used to have girls come up to me wherever I was and flirt with me. They expected me to act in a way. I couldn't be gentle. I was supposed to be rough and cruel. The girls wanted someone to dominate someone."

"Women like to be dominated. Don't you want a woman at your feet?"

"Mrs. Montgomery, the only thing I want at my feet is my shoes."

"Samuel, did you ever find the pleasure of a woman?"

"Yes, I had sex, but it wasn't from love, but it was very one sided. Yet I had to keep the facade of caring about the girl."

"But wasn't sex fun?"

"Not as fun with a guy, it's not as tight."

"Why don't you have anal sex with a woman?"

"Mother, both Bunny and I have had sex with a woman, but for us it wasn't fulfilling. Neither of us like to play the game."

"Surely men play games too."

"We must to an extent, but it it's a lot more honest of a relationship."

"Mother, I don't really care to talk about this anymore."

"It is because down deep you are ashamed."

"Mrs. Mont…"

"You two just need to find the right woman, that's all. A woman who isn't surface level."

"Mother, what do you do with yourself these days?"

"I read a lot, listen to music, sometimes I go out and see the town."

"How is it different from the old days? You left Twin Oaks a week before the takeover. Have your suppliers been friendly? Did you seek them out?"

"No, they all came one after another. I didn't ask for help. They each told me that they wanted to keep me in good spirits. I don't know why they all wanted to serve me."

"You were prime minister. They decided you were gonna be leader after they took over."

"Oh, come on. How do you even know these men?"

"Paul Kopach and Ivan Doss used to be two of your suitors after Dad died, right?"

"Well, yes."

"As a matter of fact, you were quite fond of Ivan Doss."

"Yes, I used to see them both. All of them are smugglers now."

"No, they're revolutionaries determined to overthrow the country."

"Come now."

"At first, they thought we white people would be easy to organize, to overthrow Nabutu. That was just a couple months when Nabutu did red and green check stuff. It made everyone jealous of their neighbor. He took a long time taking away everyone's property. But did you see he tried to make people jealous of each other? It caused hostility among whites."

"Well, you could be right."

"The three tried to think of how they would plan a spearhead. After the first year, they figured out the military force is too concentrated in area, that would be the points of attack. They worked long and hard, all for naught. Then their brain power was planning how they could sabotage the government."

"They couldn't find figure out how to do it."

"No, again, the army and Nabutu had everything planned out."

"How do you know so much about what the underground has been doing?"

"What do you think I have been doing for the past three years?"

"As soon as you left home?"

"No, after the takeover."

"How about you Samuel?"

"I joined two years ago. I was a messenger for a lower parliament committee."

"What committee?"

"Committee 110, the regulation for over-the-counter drugs, I was on the laxative committee."

"Laxative? All day I've heard gross things, Samuel."

"Why is this conversation too strong for your mother? To tell the truth, for some people laxatives don't do a damn bit of good."

"What? Come on Bunny. I've taken some stuff and it doesn't work for two minutes and then the bombs come."

"Well Richard, it's a disease that has afflicted a few blacks. The change of lifestyle from tribal life to modern style, it is known as white death."

"Badon, when are you coming out of the toilet?"

"As soon as I take a crap."

"Badon, after that meal you're still having that trouble?"

"Yes dear. Dear, I have to do some thinking, so don't bother me."

It all started just as a compromise. They all wanted to torture the whites, to free themselves. They wanted another Nazi regime. Since as far back as I can remember, I've always liked white people. I didn't hate them for being white but for the oppression they stood for. Those old underground days, when we would overthrow whitey. But their police state was always just a little too tight. Then Montgomery took over. The revolution was to go off a year after she was in office. Yet she calmed the country and changed social mores, to think what she had to put up from the whites. The fire of the revolution was quenched. The country was more relaxed. But we, the hardcore still wanted revolution. Think if we had gone on with it that year, I probably wouldn't be here now. Surely, I wouldn't be here now, if not for those right-wing fools who voted out Montgomery. I remember how my plan for revolution got accepted. It's such a struggle to support a way you don't believe in. It was such a game of what things I had to say, what games to play, just to be acknowledged as a leader and after the revolution when I found out I had to punish the whites. I just gave in and decided maybe I could control them, but I guess controlling them has curtailed the rebellion. Yet now I am considered a criminal by every nation in the world for something I never did. Who poisoned the white's water? No nation protested when the whites lost their material possessions. I guess the world thought karma was returning. The idea of turning white against white was really a stroke of genius. How I wanted to have a government more civil than Montgomery's. Where people lived together. Yet it wasn't or isn't possible here. The idea of a government just trying to succeed economically and artistically. I don't want a nation run on business. I want people living a little more comfortably and people to get into creative writing, drawing, making beautiful buildings, creating. I cannot even think of a state of creation with this foolish game, I'm the oppressor now.

Richard leaned back in the leather chair. A girl's face appeared in his mind. She had short choppy red hair. Her eyes kept on getting bigger in his mind, bright blue pools. He tensely recoiled in his chair. Her name was Louise. She was the first girl he had slept with, the only girl he had slept with. He pictured himself being helped inside her; it took so long. She wouldn't help him,

"Richard," she purred, "You put it in."

He took his left hand and tried to force his head up her rug. Half the head would go in the hole and then his penis would bend out. His penis would rise a fraction of an inch; he kept trying.

"Luther, did you read the paper?"

"Do I ever read the paper?"

"Dad, can't you see how worried I am?"

"Yes woman," (his daughter).

She threw him the paper.

"He's bluffing I'm not leaving."

"But they'll kill us."

"They have to be bluffing."

"Daddy, don't you care about me?"

"Little girl, I was born here and I'm gonna die here."

"Badon, I want you. How could you turn me away? Why don't you love me anymore?"

"I still do."

"Okay, why are you pushing my hand away?"

"I don't want to make love."

"What are you talking about? Who are you seeing?"

"No one, dear. I only make love to you, dear."

"Will you stop masturbating and make love to me?"

"I do make love when I want to. I just don't want to now."

She puts her breast to the back of his head, "Doesn't that feel nice?"

"I don't want to."

"Look, you're still hard."

"Why did you tell me to stop the idea of overthrowing? I can continue with my group. Why don't you arrest us? You hold the white people in a prison of plywood."

"I don't understand why you came," Nabutu said

"Every time I have ever said to the ADN, 'Your government must be overthrown,' every time, every next day a man in a white suit, pure white comes up to me and tells me, 'Please don't entertain such ideas or vile thoughts.' How many spies do you have?"

"Not many."

"Dangerous government that controls the people's moods."

"What do you mean?"

"What do I mean? There is no way in heck that I will consider a revolution, but I'm begging you please stop poisoning the white people's water."

"God damn it, I haven't poisoned their water."

"Right."

"Fuck you, don't listen to those newscasts. Newscasts are bullshit."

"Don't you know we made a pact? Armstrong was the leader, remember?"

"No, this isn't his government."

"You never listened too well. What about the plans we gave you?"

"We carried those out. Damn it, you are an important man in this nation. You are the director of business management for this nation. Don't you think I care about you?"

"Why don't you ever confide in me?"

"Well, I don't talk to anyone."

"I know, God damn it, you do something with your time. What is it?"

"Research."

"Research or what? You know, you're weird. I've always known it. The nations of the world will overthrow your government before the citizens can. Please, take the poison out of the white people's water."

"Evening Red."

"Hiya Tex."

"Too bad the Broncs lost, Red. The orange was crushed, hey hey."

"Ya, the cowboys whipped it to them."

"Right Red. It's great. The best team won, that's America. A good bunch of guys fighting it out and whupping each other's ass."

"Ya Tex, America didn't get great cuz of pussies."

"Pussy is only good when it's a woman. Big Red, I have had lot of ass."

"You know Tex, talking about ass reminds me of the Nabutu fellow's wife."

"Doesn't she have a pretty pair?"

"Nice ass too."

"Ya, too bad she is married to such a dick"

"Ya, I'll say. It's time for us to get a hard on, and fuck with Nabutu. His country has all that good stuff and they're holding back on us. It's time we whupped some ass."

"Badon, I feel time is up. Why have you been so stubborn, It's imminent the world powers are ready to attack."

"They can't attack at the same time."

"You never understand, never. You never have understood. Look at all the materials we have. Don't you understand we can't afford to play around anymore? We must give raw material to all sides desiring it."

Seven old, bald oriental men were sitting around a table. All looking at each other, one the man with the long thin drooping mustache with ends that hung down like ponytails.

"We open the cookies now."

The seven simultaneously bent down and their cookies each with a pensive hopeful look.

The seventh pointed to the man on his right, "You must start. Does everyone remember the procedure?"

Everyone nodded in consent.

The first one was a burly man with fat cheeks, the largest part of the face shaped like an apple. "A land of great mineral resources," he said. "

"We know where the fortune falls."

"Hush, foolish one, never interpret a fortune in the beginning."

The next person read, "A problem is here. It must be dealt with."

All heads except the master nodded together.

"A joke at one time is not, what is something to fight for."

"Fortunes stay in the east."

"A home is where your oxen eat grass."

The last two men signaled they had no fortunes in their cookies.

All the men were pondering the meaning of the fortunes.

"We know what we must do," the master said.

All the men clapped and bowed.

The master continued, "Fine, now eat the cookie."

"Dad, have you ever seen rain like this?"

"Sure son, it always rains here."

"Two weeks in a row?"

"Honey, it's always rained. I remember one year, every home game it rained, drizzled, and the field was muddy."

"Sure, wasn't that the second championship year Vicky Willa?"

"Yes, it even snowed for a while early in that season. I wish it would have kept on. The rain will eventually stop."

"I'm tired of staying in."

"I'm tired of it too."

"Are you being a pain to your mother?"

"No, sir."

"Go out more. Don't bring your friends over, son."

"I've only had my friends over three times this week."

"Get out of the house. Leave your mother some peace."

"Roger, not only has your son been a pain to his mother, but he threw a snowball at a bus."

"Stay out of trouble, son."

"Why can't you be more like Marcia?" her mom said.

"What do you mean?" the son said.

"Marcia goes out to see her friends," Mother said.

"I told you not to mess with boys yet."

"Marcia sees her friends."

"What friends?"

"Jenny, Cindy, Cathi, Don..."

"If you get knocked up, little girl, you're out on your own."

Leftwinger DiArgentine takes the ball. He's got a break away. DiArgentine one on one against goalie Johnstone. Iron has passed the penalty box. Johnstone is coming out to cut the angle. DiArgentine cocks his left foot. Johnstone dives. Diargentine steps over the ball, He's dribbling. He's got an open net. Johnstone is still down. He's not getting up. Williams is the closest player to Iron. Iron's dribbling the ball into the goal, shoot, Iron, shoot. He doesn't see Williams. Iron is practically in the goal now. Williams dives. DiArgentine falls no foul is called. Williams clears the ball towards Issacs Richter. He heads the ball out of bounds. Play has been stopped at Calverton. The home fans are furious over the rough tackle on DiArgentine.

"Excuse me, Roger. I was watching Williams sprinting down to make the tackle. I believe he got the ball and DiArgentine fell over trying to get the foul."

"Phil, the instant replay is being shown on the score board.

"Williams had a good angle. He dove off his right leg, he twisted in mid-air, and got the ball before the man. Definitely a clean play. Williams was the Relton player who took the shot, Andreas saved it, two-fisted, to Langstrom who passed it to DiArgentine, who was playing almost at the mid-field stripe. In this dead-locked game, Williams sprinted down field after his shot. He covered a lot of ground blocking that shot."

"Indeed, he did. What makes that play even more important is that Johnstone still hasn't gotten up. Right now, they are bringing in the stretcher. It appears from here that it is an ankle injury. With Johnstone on the ground DiArgentine thought he had all day. He never saw Williams coming. With the injury time out, we'll break to a commercial, the score Relton 0 Calverton 0."

Richard was speaking out loud to himself, mother Mary, and Bunny, who happened to be in the same room.

At first, they thought we white people would be easy to organize to overthrow Nabutu. That was just a couple years ago when Nabutu did that red and green check stuff. It made everyone jealous of their neighbor. He took a long time taking everyone's property, but did you see how he tried to make people jealous of each other? It caused hostility among whites

They tried to think of how they would plan a spearhead after the first year. They decided Nabutu's military was too concentrated where they wanted to attack. They worked long and hard all for naught. Then their brain power was planning how they could sabotage the government. They couldn't figure out how to do it, not again. The army and Nabutu had everything planned out.

"Other nations reactioned to internal affairs of this nation. This nation, as you should know, was primarily a nation that achieved economic parity by selling its natural resources. We have shifted our economy to a more self-sufficient nature of economics for an emerging nation. My point is that other nations desire these materials. This has been shown by several innuendos aimed against our nation. Originally, it was intended for some nations to use force to coerce a change in government. Fortunately, intelligence units of this country have snuffed out possible parties in this nation. For nations that want to consider invading, we will know when you want to attack. When we changed the system of government, we therefore took precautions against attack by other nations. Many nations have condemned us because of our moral situation of the whites. Unfortunately, you don't take into account the ill treatment of our ancestors, up to my generation."

"Badon, I feel the time is up. Why have you been so stubborn? It's imminent that the world powers are ready to attack."

"They can't all attack at the same time."

"You never understand, never. You never understood. Look at all the materials we have. Don't you understand we can't afford to play around anymore? We must give and sell raw material to all sides desiring it."

"I didn't know if it was a movie happening, These three superpowers, the many years... What if all I had done, still wanted, and haven't yet done is the way it is supposed to be. There are still tribes in the mudulaw. Abolish old, outdated laws and ideals, and teach and intellectualize, and what of instinct and first impression, all this financial dickering, the making of an economy."

"I hope everyone everywhere can hear me."

Mary Montgomery turned out to her window and saw nothing unusual.

"I am Prime Minister Nabutu. Speakers have been placed so every citizen of our nation can hear what I have to say. If you would like to watch me, channels 5, 9, and 13 have given me permission to appear on them. On radio, you can listen to me on bands 4, 5, 7, 8, 11, 13, and 15. I would like to thank the owners of these various stations for letting me have the privilege of being on their stations. Various times in the past week, I've tried to get the message across that I didn't have any part of poisoning the reservoirs. The white people's reservoirs. Nobody, even my brothers, various leaders in the government to independent citizens, no one has believed me. For the last two days, piping has been placed for every citizen of this nation to drink from the municipal reservoirs. These reservoirs will be the source of all water for everyone in this nation. As you see in these movies, this the national engineering company connecting lines from the Olympic reservoir to the town of Elizabethtown."

"Our water isn't poisoned," Richard said

"The water of Elizabethtown from the Ganges reservoir is thought to been pure. Our best scientists still conclude the water is pure. But we are not playing with the citizens' lives in Dorchester.

Every province's major reservoir has been connected to the system. While the poisoned water centers have been closed.

Three earthquakes occurred today, in opposite parts of the world. In the Binded Being of Vespucci, Bear Land, and Mao Land, below the Being of Diego, an area zoned for a water purification plant is where the tectonic event happened. Scientists are stunned that no tremors had been recorded prior to the earthquakes. If you hadn't figured the different time zones, these earthquakes happened at the exact same time."

Nabutu had neutralized foreign adversaries. Mary Montgomery, her son and his lover finally moved to another nation. Most of the whites were gone. The white underground was more invisible than before. The economy was on the way up. People had more things than before. And of course, the trouble was just about to begin.